Hot, Spicy Murder

Papa Pacelli's Pizzeria Series

Book Twenty-Seven

By

Patti Benning

Author's Note: On the next page, you'll find out how to access all of my books easily, as well as locate books by best-selling author, Summer Prescott. I'd love to hear your thoughts on my books, the storylines, and anything else that you'd like to comment on – reader feedback is very important to me. Please see the following page for my publisher's contact information. If you'd like to be on her list of "folks to contact" with updates, release and sales notifications, etc...just shoot her an email and let her know. Thanks for reading!

Also...

...if you're looking for more great reads, from me and Summer, check out the Summer Prescott Publishing Book Catalog:

http://summerprescottbooks.com/book-catalog/ for some truly delicious stories.

Contact Info for Summer Prescott Publishing:

Twitter: @summerprescott1

Blog and Book Catalog:

http://summerprescottbooks.com

Email: summer.prescott.cozies@gmail.com

And…look up The Summer Prescott Fan Page and Summer Prescott Publishing Page on Facebook – let's be friends!

To sign up for our fun and exciting newsletter, which will give you opportunities to win prizes and swag, enter contests, and be the first to know about New Releases, click here: https://forms.aweber.com/form/02/1682036 602.htm

Table of Contents

Hot, Spicy Murder

Papa Pacelli's Pizzeria Series

Book Twenty-Seven

Chapter One

Eleanora Ward felt like crying. It was the end of what she was sure had been the busiest week of her life, and in just over eight hours, she was supposed to be on an airplane flying towards Florida. The only problem was, she hadn't even started packing. Between the never-ending stream of customers at the pizzeria, the hassle of her and Russell trying to organize the new house that they had just bought, and with both of them juggling work and trying to find enough time to go shopping for furniture together, she had been too exhausted to even think about her trip to Florida.

And now, of course, she was faced with the monumental task of packing everything that she needed for a week in the sun in one suitcase. The task wasn't made any easier by the fact that most of her summer clothes were still packed away in a box in the back of the closet at the Pacelli house next door, but her suitcase and all her toiletries were here in her and Russell's new house.

"I'd better get started," she said out loud.

Bunny, her black and white papillon, perked her ears up. Ellie paused to stroke the soft fur on the dog's head, glad for a moment that her husband, Russell, was staying behind for the trip. While she would have loved Russell's company, it was a relief to know that he would be watching the animals. She always felt bad upsetting their lives when they had to go to a pet sitter. Marlowe, especially, seemed to take it roughly. The big green and red parrot wasn't a fan of change and liked very few people besides Ellie herself.

It didn't take her long to pack her toiletry bag, which simply entailed moving her supplies from the bathroom cabinet to the waterproof bag. Anything she forgot she could easily replace, so she hardly bothered double-checking it. More important was her laptop, and her charging cords for the computer and her cell phone. She had traveled to Florida so often in the past year that it was beginning to feel routine, and it didn't take her much time to finish packing everything that she could.

She zipped up her suitcase and went downstairs to find Sawyer, the black Labrador retriever puppy, taking a nap on the couch. He no longer needed to be directly supervised all the time, but she still didn't trust him in the house alone. Luckily, he was all too happy to accompany her across the lawn to the Pacelli house, so with him at her heels, she dragged the suitcase through the grass, all the while mentally berating herself for not remembering to move the boxes of clothing over sooner.

When she opened the door to the Pacelli house, she felt an unexpected blast of nostalgia. It didn't look much different; most of her belongings had been upstairs, so aside from Marlowe's cage in the hallway, no large items had been removed, but the house already had the air of emptiness about it.

She wondered, not for the first time, whether her grandmother would be pleased with this arrangement. She and Russell had decided to have the new house be a surprise for Nonna, but every now and then, Ellie got the urge to tell her anyway. It was going to be a big change for all of them, though not as big as it might have been. Finding a house right next door to her grandmother for her and Russell to live in had really been the perfect blessing. Rationally, she knew that they would not get a chance like this again, and that of course her grandmother would have encouraged them to make the most of the opportunity if she had been there.

She and Russell had agreed to tell Nonna about the house the instant they got back from Florida. They had already installed a two-way intercom system between the houses, so if Nonna needed to talk to them, or they wanted to check on her, they would be just the press of a button away. And besides, Ellie couldn't deny that she was looking forward to having her own home with her husband. It was the beginning of a whole new world for both them.

Since all of her summer clothes had been packed away neatly, it didn't take her long to pack what she needed for her trip into the suitcase. When she got back, she could just unpack them in the closet at the new house. It would be summer here in Maine soon enough, and she was already looking forward to the warm days ahead.

Back in her and Russell's new house, Ellie took a moment to pass Marlowe an almond in the shell through the bars, then went into the kitchen to feed the dogs. She was supposed to be going to bed soon;

she had to wake up early to drive down to Portland to catch her flight, but she wanted to wait for Russell to get home. She wasn't going to see her husband for nearly a week after this, and after spending every day together for the past couple of months, that was going to be rough.

While she waited, she scrolled through her emails on her phone, double and triple checking her flight time and departure gate, and then re-reading her last email to Linda, which the other woman had yet to answer. The Florida pizzeria had been through a major upheaval recently, and she had been micromanaging the business more than usual — at least, as well as she could while living in Maine. It would be good to visit the pizzeria again and make sure that everything was going well, but she would have to remember her promise to her grandmother not to work too much while she was down there. This trip was meant for the two of them to spend time together; she could always make a work trip later.

The dogs ran to the front door a moment before Ellie heard the sound of Russell's truck pulling up the driveway. She put her phone down, glancing in the hall mirror as she walked toward the door. Even though they had been married and living together for a few months, she still got butterflies in her stomach whenever her husband got home after a long day. Some days it was hard to believe that she was married, and that this man she loved would be there every day for the rest of her life.

Smiling at her reflection, she turned to hurry down the hall, eager to see Russell and get in some last goodbyes before she went to bed.

Chapter Two

It was still morning when her plane landed in Florida. Ellie had fallen asleep during the flight and was disoriented when she woke up as the plane began to descend. It had been dark out when she had flown out of Portland, and the feeling of not knowing what time it was, was unsettling.

She got her bearings about her quickly enough and was feeling wide-awake by the time people began getting off the plane. The trips to Florida were familiar, and she didn't even have to check the signs in the airport to know that she was heading the right direction to pick up her luggage. It was a simple matter to find her suitcase and make her way to the other side of the airport where the office for the rental cars was. She smiled to herself as she paid for the vehicle and accepted the keys. The first time she had come down here, everything had been so confusing, and she had gotten lost in the airport more times than she could count. This familiarity was nice, and it was also a reminder of how much her life had changed.

The roads surrounding the airport were always busy, though they weren't as bad today as they had been in the past, since it was a weekday morning. Still, she never enjoyed driving through Miami, and didn't begin to relax until she reached the outskirts of the city.

The retirement community her grandmother had lived in for the past six months was on the coast just outside of Miami, and coincidentally was only a short drive to the Florida pizzeria. If she took only a small detour, she would drive right past the restaurant. Ellie hesitated for a moment at the intersection but decided to head straight to her grandmother's. It was still early enough in the morning that no one would be at Papa Pacelli's, and there was no real reason she needed to stop by an empty restaurant. She would get plenty of time to visit later this week and see how Linda was holding up.

Her favorite part of the drive from the airport to her grandmother's was the last stretch, when the road hugged the coast and she got to enjoy the scenery of the beaches, the ocean, the palm trees, and the various shops and houses. Even though she lived a stone's throw from the ocean in Maine, the two great bodies of water could not have been more different. In Maine, the ocean was cold and choppy, and the water was usually a dark, steel grey color. The beaches were rocky, and only the bravest people swam in the warmest months.

Down here in Florida, the ocean was a gorgeous dark blue, and the beaches were sandy and dotted with swimmers and sunbathers. *I don't blame Nonna for wanting to spend winter down here,* she thought. Her grandmother had spent decades suffering through the cold, brutal Maine winters, and Ellie knew that she had only done it out of love for her grandfather. The warm Florida weather and the active city were the perfect match for her independent grandmother.

At last, she saw the sign at the entrance to the community and turned on her blinker. The subdivision felt oddly empty as she drove through it, and she realized that a lot of the residents must only stay for the winter months. She knew that the condominium did six-month leases, though some of the residents lived there full-time as well.

She drove slowly through the twisting streets until she saw her grandmother's condominium in the distance. She had to double check the address; her grandmother couldn't drive, but nonetheless there was an expensive looking bright yellow sports car in the driveway. She had called her grandmother as soon as she had disembarked from the plane, and the older woman hadn't mentioned any guests, but she figured it was possible that one of Nonna's friends had stopped by without warning. Ellie parked along the street, not wanting to block the other car from leaving the driveway. She shot the vehicle an admiring glance as she walked past it, dragging her suitcase. She knew that a lot of the people in this retirement community were well off, but it was still strange to see such a flashy car in a community where many of the residents couldn't drive at all.

She knocked on the front door, already grinning. She was excited to see her grandmother, even though it had only been a few of months since the last time they had seen each other. She felt a moment of doubt once again as she thought about the surprise that she and Russell had for the older woman, but forced it down. Everything would turn out well, she was sure of it.

The door opened a moment later, and Ellie and her grandmother beamed at each other for a moment before rushing into a hug. Ellie squeezed the older woman as tightly as she dared, glad that her grandmother didn't feel as if she had lost any weight. The white-haired woman was tan and looked healthy, even better than she had the summer before. It made Ellie's heart beat a bit easier in her chest. Her grandmother was in her mid-eighties, and even though it was sometimes easy to forget how old she was, Ellie was always worried that her age would catch up to her. She didn't know what she would do without the older woman in her life.

"Come on in," Nonna said. "I just made some fresh lemonade, and I thought we could go out for brunch if you'd like. I can't imagine that you had a good breakfast on the plane."

"Brunch sounds wonderful," Ellie said. "I'd like to sit down for a few minutes first, though. I slept on the plane, but I still feel tired. I don't know why travel always takes so much out of me."

"Come and sit down in the kitchen, then," Nonna said. "We have so much to talk about. I'm glad you're finally here."

Amused at her grandmother's eager, bustling energy, Ellie relented and left her suitcase by the front door, slipping off her sandals and padding barefoot across the lush carpet toward the bright and airy kitchen. Despite the heat outside, or maybe because of it, the house was chilly. The Pacelli house in Maine was old, and didn't have central air, and she was amused to realize that her grandmother took full advantage of the top-of-the-line air conditioning in the condo. Her grandmother might love the sun and warm weather, but she still preferred to have a cool house to retreat back into when it all got to be a bit much.

"How was the trip, dear?" her grandmother asked as she bustled around the kitchen, removing clean glasses from the cupboard and taking the pitcher of freshly made lemonade out of the fridge.

"I slept for most of the flight," Ellie said. "The drive was pleasant, though. This really is a beautiful area." She sipped the lemonade, which was just perfect – not too sweet, and not too sour. The color reminded her of the bright yellow car sitting in the driveway. "Is someone here?"

Her grandmother frowned. "No, it's just me. I told all my friends you were coming today, so I don't think any of them are planning on stopping by. Why do you ask?"

"The car in the driveway…" Ellie frowned, getting more confused. "Whose is it?"

To her surprise, her grandmother grinned. "There's something I need to tell you. It all happened so fast, you see. I probably should have spoken to you first, but I know you've been so busy these past few days, and I figured you probably wouldn't mind too much. You know my friend Grace Elliott in Kittiport? Her husband purchased the car last week and was going to have someone drive it up to Maine for him, but that didn't work out, so she called me and asked if you and I can drive it up when we come back home. It will take a couple of days, but it should be fun, I haven't been on a road trip in such a long time. And of course, you would get to drive the car."

Ellie blinked. It was a lot to take in. She had been planning on staying for nearly a week, then flying back with her grandmother, but now it seemed that plans had changed unexpectedly. She imagined driving the beautiful convertible up along the East Coast, and grinned.

"I'm glad I spent the extra money on exchangeable tickets," she said. "You're right, this is a surprise, but a good one. A road trip will be fun."

Her grandmother smiled. "That's what I was hoping you would say. I figure we can leave Wednesday, that should give us plenty of time to get home on schedule. Or we could leave earlier, if you want to sightsee along the way."

"I came out here to spend time with you, so as long as you're happy, we can leave anytime. I do want to stop by the pizzeria first and say hi to Linda, but after that, I'm all yours for the week. Now that I know we're going to be driving it, I'm going to go outside and take a couple of pictures of the car to send to Russell." Ellie smiled, thinking about how jealous her husband would be. He drove an old truck with four-wheel-drive, which was useful for the sometimes-icy Maine roads, but he appreciated flashy sports cars just as much as the next man.

"I can't believe I'm going to be going home," Nonna said, raising her lemonade glass. "I can't wait to spend the next six months up north. I hope you'll tell me about everything that's happened since I left, but first, let's decide where we want to get brunch. I don't know about you, but I'm starving."

Chapter Three

The two of them decided to stay in Florida for the next day, and leave early the morning after to begin their road trip. That gave Ellie enough time to visit the pizzeria and check on Linda and the others, and also relax at the beach for a while. She didn't mind that her grandmother had changed their plans suddenly without talking to her, and if anything, it made her feel a little bit better about the surprise that she and Russell had planned for Nonna when they got back. Besides, a road trip really would be fun. She flew back and forth a lot, but she hadn't gotten a chance to see much of the country. Now, she would be driving all the way from one of the southernmost states to one of the northernmost ones, and she was looking forward to the adventure.

Of course, she had packed for a weeklong stay in Florida, not a week long drive up the coast, but luckily many of the same things that were comfortable to wear while lounging around in the sun were also comfortable to wear whilst sitting in the car. She knew that she would be the one driving the entire way; her grandmother no longer had her license, so even if Ellie got tired, the older woman wouldn't be able to take over.

That evening, they went to dinner at the pizzeria. She had already emailed Linda, and the other woman knew to expect her, so they were greeted at the door by an exuberant, if stressed looking, familiar face.

"It's good to see you again," Linda said, surprising Ellie by pulling her into a hug. "Sit wherever you want. What can I get the two of you to drink?"

"I'll have a water," Ellie said. It was hot outside, and with the sun beating down on her, she was beginning to feel parched.

"I'd like the strawberry banana smoothie," Nonna declared. Ellie smiled. The smoothies were a new addition to the menu. They had decided to try them out down in Florida, where the demand for them would be greater, and if things went well, she was planning on introducing them to the menu at the Maine pizzeria for the summer.

"Coming right up," Linda said. Ellie watched as her friend hurried away, feeling the slightest twinge of worry. Linda had definitely lost weight since the last time she had seen her. Ellie knew that she was dealing with a lot, and she just hoped that her friend didn't overwork herself.

Ellie and Nonna took a seat at a booth near the register. Nonna was happily chatting about all of the things she planned to do when they got back to Maine. Ellie was only half listening; the other half of her was looking around the restaurant, trying not to be too obvious as she evaluated how well the place was doing.

She had to hand it to Linda; even though the other woman was going through a lot, the place was spotlessly clean, and all of the guests seemed happy. One of the employees, a young woman whom Ellie hardly knew, was taking an order from a family with two small children. She was glad to see that the young woman was smiling courteously, even when one of the children accidentally spilled a cup of water.

"Here are your drinks," Linda said. "Are you sure we can't get you something else, Ellie?"

"Thanks, but I'll just have the water for now. I know I'll get a headache if I don't drink enough of it, especially in this heat."

"Well, just let me know if you change your mind. The smoothies have been extremely popular. You should try one, at least."

"Maybe I'll get one to go after we're done eating," Ellie said. "So, what's the special today?"

"Spicy shrimp pizza on a flat bread crust," Linda said. "It's served cold. It's been pretty popular; it was a special a couple of weeks ago, and we decided to bring it back. Everyone loves it."

"I'll have two slices of that," Ellie said.

"I'll have the same," Nonna said. "I remember the last time you guys served it, you're right. It is pretty good."

Linda beamed at her, then hurried off to go and get their orders ready. Ellie leaned back in the booth, satisfied that the restaurant wasn't about to burst into flames or crumble into a heap of rubble. She didn't like to admit how worried she had been about Linda. Sandra, one of Linda's close friends and the assistant manager at the pizzeria, had passed away during Ellie's last visit to Florida. She could only imagine how hard it was for Linda to run this place on her own.

"So, do you still come here often?" Ellie asked her grandmother.

"Of course," her grandmother said. "It reminds me of home. And you just can't beat the food or the service here. You did well in choosing Linda to run the pizzeria   for   you."

"I know I did," Ellie said. She smiled. "She's been through a lot, but she seems to be doing all right, doesn't she?"

"She's managing," Nonna said. "She's a survivor, that one. Plus, I think it helps her to have this place. It gives her something to focus on."

Ellie could understand that. She sipped her ice-cold water and smiled. It was reassuring to see Linda again face-to-face, and it was a good reminder that no matter how bad things got, life always went on.

After dinner, they returned to the rental car company, so Ellie could drop the vehicle off, then took a taxi back to the condominium complex. The next morning, they got up before the sun began to come up. It took them a while to double and triple check that Nonna had everything she wanted to bring with her. It was tough to fit all of their luggage into the tiny car, but somehow, they managed. Ellie waited patiently as her grandmother took one last look around the condo that had been her home for the past six months, and she could tell that the other woman found it bittersweet to be leaving.

"You'll see it again in October," she reminded her grandmother.

"I know. And I want to get home." She took one last look down the hall, and then stepped inside to join Ellie on the front porch and lock the door.

Ellie took the seat behind the driver's wheel and began fiddling with the car keys. It took her a moment to realize that there wasn't a key – not a physical one, at least. Instead, there was a button near the steering wheel that she had to push to start the engine. It was strange to hear the car purr to life at the touch of a button.

"This is making me feel old," Ellie said. "You don't even need a key to start a car anymore."

"I'm glad I'm not the one driving," her grandmother said. "This machine frightens me."

Ellie was glad that her first experience with the car was on the slow, empty streets of the retirement community, because it took her a while to adjust to the sensitive steering and gas pedal. By the time they reached the office, she was grinning. This was going to be a fun road trip – as long as she didn't somehow manage to crash the car.

Indeed, driving up along the Florida coast with the roof down and the wind blowing in her hair was an amazing experience that left both women laughing and happy. They drove for most of the day, stopping occasionally for bathroom breaks, and once to eat lunch at a lovely little restaurant right next to a beautiful beach. Ellie leaned back in her chair after finishing her fish taco and sighed. While it wasn't exactly the week that she had planned for, she was definitely enjoying the road trip. Her grandmother was too, she thought, but she could tell that the older woman was beginning to get uncomfortable from sitting in the vehicle for so long.

After taking a slow walk on the beach to stretch their legs and help them digest, the two of them folded themselves back into the vehicle and took off again. It was getting dark by the time Ellie mentioned finding a hotel for the night, and they were already well into Georgia by then.

"Let's pull over soon so I can look up local hotels online," Ellie said. Her grandmother agreed, and they got off at the next rest stop. Ellie pulled out her cell phone, then sighed. "I don't have any cell phone service here. We can keep driving for a bit, if you'd like, and see if my phone picks up the signal again, or we could just get off at the next exit that promises lodging."

"My vote is for the second option," her grandmother said, her eyes sparkling. "This is supposed to be an adventure, isn't it? So, let's just see where life takes us."

Chapter Four

The very next exit promised both lodging and fuel, so Ellie took it even though it seemed that they were far from any city. She had her doubts and the ramp ended on a quiet country road, but they followed the signs that pointed them toward the promised motel.

"This really is out in the middle of nowhere," Nonna said. She didn't look worried; on the contrary, she looked excited. Ellie realized that her grandmother must have missed the peace and quiet of living outside of town – her retirement community was a busy place, and they were only a short drive from a very major city. *It must be good for her to get out of town for a while,* Ellie thought.

"I just hope they have a vacancy," Ellie said. "I'm getting sick of driving."

The motel turned out to be only a few miles down the road, on the outskirts of one of the tiniest towns that Ellie had ever seen. Luckily, the word vacancy was flashing on the large sign that read Maple's Motel. Right next to the motel was a small diner that already looked closed for the night, and kitty corner across the intersection was a ramshackle gas station with a tow truck that read Rob's Vehicle Repair in the parking lot. Ellie was having her doubts about staying in this motel for the night – it looked just as rundown as everything else in the tiny town did – but her grandmother seemed up for the adventure, so she turned into the parking lot. She still wasn't used to driving the sleek, shiny car, and accidentally hit the brakes too hard, jerking them to a stop in one of the parking places.

"Shall I go in on my own?" she asked. "I can get us a room, and I'll see if they offer breakfast in the mornings."

"I'm happy to wait here," her grandmother said. "It will be easier than trying to get in and out of this car." Ellie nodded, understanding. The car had a very low seat, and it was difficult for her grandmother to get up from it.

"I'll be right back," she promised, leaving the vehicle running. She grabbed her purse and went inside, looking around the small lobby. It appeared to be empty, but the door had been unlocked, and lights were on inside, so she assumed that they must be open. She approached the front desk and rang the bell that was on it.

She waited a moment, but no one showed up. She was about to press the bell again when she heard the murmur of voices behind the door. The sign on the door read *Laundry Room*, so she figured it would be all right if she peeked inside. She pushed her way through it, then quickly stumbled back, gasping out, "I'm so sorry."

She had walked in on two people kissing passionately. Both of them jumped when she came into the room, and she felt embarrassed. She let the door close behind her, then turned to the front desk, where she was surprised to see that an older woman had appeared.

"How can I help you, dear?" she asked. Behind her, Ellie heard the door to the laundry room open. Out of the corner of her eye, she saw a man with a clipboard walk through the door to the parking lot. The woman walked around Ellie to the other side of the desk, standing next to the older woman with a flush on her cheeks.

"I'd like to rent a room," Ellie said, putting the incident out of her mind. "My grandmother and I will be staying for the night."

"Just the one night?"

"Yes. We'll be leaving pretty early in the morning."

"Okay. Check out time is eleven, just in case you decide to sleep late. We don't serve breakfast here, but the diner next door opens at seven. Will you be paying with cash or credit? We don't accept checks."

"I'll be paying with my card," Ellie said, digging her wallet out of her purse.

"You're all set. You'll be in room number eleven. Here are the keys. Just drop them off here in the morning when you leave. My name is Annie Maple, by the way, but you can call me Annie. I'll probably be the one here when you check out."

"Thanks," Ellie said. "I'll see you in the morning, I'm sure."

She made her way back to the car, her eyes counting down the numbers on the exterior doors. She had already almost forgotten the incident with the man and the woman in the laundry room. It really wasn't any of her business, she was just embarrassed that she had walked in on such a passionate embrace.

Purely by coincidence, she had parked almost directly in front of room number eleven, so she simply reached in and shut off the car, then went around to the passenger side to open her grandmother's door and helped the older woman out.

The room wasn't anything special. There were two neatly made beds, a microwave, and a small bathroom with a questionable tub. Still, it was dark and cool inside, and as she sat down on the corner of her bed, she sighed in relief. It felt good not to be driving. They still had quite a few hours of their trip left, but she was sure that she would feel more up to continuing to drive after a good night's sleep.

"Are you hungry?" she asked after her grandmother came out of the bathroom.

"A little bit, but I think I'd like to lay down before we find somewhere to eat," the older woman said.

"Okay." Ellie was tempted to do the same, but she knew that once she lay down, she wouldn't want to get back up. Instead, she decided to make herself useful. "I'm going to go and get some ice and see where the vending machines are. Whenever you're ready, we can head back out and see if we can find a restaurant that's open this late."

"Will you shut the curtains before you go out?"

"Of course."

Ellie grabbed the ice bucket and a plastic liner for it, and, making sure that she had her key, slipped out of the room. Her stomach rumbled, and she patted her pockets to make sure that she had a couple of dollar bills available. If she found vending machines, she was going to stop and get a small snack. She didn't know when her grandmother might wake up, and for all she knew, there weren't any restaurants open past ten in the area, so if she could find something to eat, she would take it.

The ice machine and vending machines were situated between one of the long arms of the motel and the front lobby. She took her time perusing the options in the vending machine, and eventually settled on a bag of chips and a small package of beef jerky. After she had her food, she filled up the ice bucket, putting the top on it before turning to head back to her room.

She hadn't gotten more than a few steps away from the machines when she heard a squeal of breaks and a loud crash coming from the parking lot. With a bad feeling in her stomach, Ellie hurried toward the sound, skidding to a halt as she stared in horror at the sleek yellow car, which had just been run into by another vehicle.

Fighting back the surge of anger that she felt when she saw the wrecked vehicle – it wasn't even hers; what would her grandmother's friend say? – she hurried forward to see if whoever had been driving the SUV was all right. She was relieved when she saw the driver undo her seatbelt and opened the driver's side door.

"Are you okay?" Ellie called out.

The woman looked up at her, but instead of responding, she just pointed. Ellie turned, following the direction of the woman's finger, and felt the bag of chips and beef jerky tumble out of her hands. Just inside the open doorway of one of the motel rooms, a man was slumped, his eyes wide and staring, and a smear of blood on the door behind him. Ellie forgot all about the car as she took a hesitant step toward the man, hoping against hope that he would move, but somehow knowing in her heart that he was already dead.

Chapter Five

She had left her cell phone in the motel room, which she realized only after patting her pockets frantically for a moment. The woman who had been in the SUV came up behind her, and Ellie saw that she already had a phone in her hands.

"I – I was just driving through the parking lot and I saw him. I was trying to figure out just what exactly I was seeing, and I must not have been paying attention to where I was going," she murmured. "Is he… dead?"

"I think so," Ellie said, still staring at the man. Summoning all of the bravery that she could find, she approached the man who was slumped against the door and pressed her fingers to his neck, but try as she might, she couldn't find a pulse. His eyes were still open, and he hadn't blinked once. Even though she tried not to look at it, the blood was only inches from her face, and she could tell that it was fresh. Whatever had happened to him, it had happened recently. She must have walked right by him on her trip to the vending machines but had been so focused on her task of finding food that she hadn't even noticed.

She heard beeping behind her, and turned to see the other woman pressing a cell phone to her ear. A moment later, she began talking rapidly to the emergency dispatcher. Ellie stood up, wiping her hand reflexively on her pants even though she hadn't done anything more than touch the man's skin. She looked at his face, frowning, wondering why it looked so familiar. It wasn't as though she knew anyone in the area. She bit her lip, tearing her eyes away from his face, only to have them land on a clipboard that had fallen to the floor beside him. Suddenly, her mind made the connection, and she gasped. This was the same man who she had seen kissing that woman in the motel's laundry room not even an hour beforehand. She felt a chill.

"The police are on their way," the woman said, her voice shaking. "Should we tell someone who works at the motel? What should we do about the body? What if someone with children walks by?"

"I'm not sure that we should do anything," Ellie said. "I'm sure the police will handle everything when they get here. How long did they say they would be?"

"Not long," the other woman said. "We should probably just wait here, you're right. We shouldn't leave the body alone, and I wouldn't feel safe waiting here by myself."

The truth was, Ellie really did not want to be left alone with the man either. For all they knew, whoever had attacked him was still around. She couldn't seem to take her eyes away from his face, and felt nausea building in her stomach. The other woman's presence was a welcome distraction.

"My name is Regina, by the way," she said. "Did you know him?"

"I saw him in the motel lobby, that's all," Ellie said.

"I've never seen a dead person before," the other woman whispered. "I don't know what to do."

"Neither do I," Ellie admitted. They both froze as a door at the other end of the building opened and a young woman came out. Ellie tensed, worried that the woman would walk by them, but she made a beeline for the parking lot and got into a vehicle. As she drove away, Ellie wondered if they should have tried to stop her. For all they knew, she might have had something to do with the attack. Wouldn't the police want to question everyone? She wished Russell was there. This was his job, after all, not hers.

"Do you hear that?" the other woman asked. Ellie fell silent, concentrating, and then relaxed slightly. Sure enough, she could hear the sound of sirens off in the distance. The police were nearly there.

"They'll know what to do," she repeated, as much to herself as to the other woman. Her palms were damp with sweat, and she wiped them on her shorts before bending down to pick up the bag of chips and jerky.

She wasn't hungry in the slightest anymore, but she couldn't very well just leave them lying on the sidewalk.

All of a sudden, she remembered Nonna. Her grandmother would be wondering where she was, and she wished that she had a way to let the other woman know that everything was okay. She wasn't looking forward to telling her grandmother about what had happened.

The sirens drew nearer, and eventually Ellie saw two ancient police vehicles with flashing red and blue lights pull into the motel's parking lot. They parked near the two crumpled cars, and shut the sirens off, though they left the lights on. The officers got out, one of them hanging back to report something into his handheld radio, and the other one approaching them.

The next half hour passed in a blur as Ellie answered what felt like the same questions over and over. The paramedics arrived and spent only a few short minutes working on the man before she heard one of them call the time of death, and they loaded him onto a stretcher before covering him with a sheet and wheeling him to the ambulance.

A moment of silence fell as the paramedics lifted the stretcher into the ambulance and shut the doors. There was something so final about it, and even the police stopped talking for a moment. Ellie wondered just how many murders they dealt with. A town this small couldn't have that much going on.

Just as the ambulance doors slammed shut, another door opened just down the sidewalk from them, and Ellie saw her grandmother's white-haired head poking out.

"Ellie, I was worried…" the older woman broke off, taking in the sight of the two police vehicles in the parking lot. "What's going on?"

"I'll explain everything soon, Nonna," Ellie said. The police seemed to be just about finished questioning them, and already had crime scene tape strung across the doorway. She heard one of them radio something back to headquarters, mentioning a forensics team.

Her grandmother frowned, but seemed about to duck back into the motel room when Ellie saw her gaze catch on the crumpled rear end of the yellow car. This time, the look on her grandmother's face was utterly horrified. She shuffled out the door and down the sidewalk, her gaze fixed on the vehicle.

"What… What…?"

"Oh, I'm so sorry," Regina said. "Was that your car?" Her wide-eyed gaze darted between Ellie and

Nonna. Ellie gave a short nod. Her grandmother was still staring at the vehicle in horror.

"We have a report that you can file with your insurance," one of the police officers said. He approached Ellie, handing her a piece of paper. "And here's my card as well. If you can think of anything that might be relevant to the case, please give me a call."

"I will," Ellie promised. He nodded, then told her that she was free to go. The other woman had been dismissed as well, and Ellie followed Regina and her grandmother over to the two vehicles. The three of them stared at the wreckage.

"I'm so sorry, ma'am," Regina was saying. "It's just that I saw the body, and I wasn't paying any attention to where I was going..."

"It's okay," her grandmother said faintly, her hands still clasped to her chest. "It's okay... we can fix it."

"My insurance should cover the whole thing," Regina said. "If you need any more information from me, just let me know."

Speechless, her grandmother simply waved the other woman away. Ellie walked up next to her, putting an arm around the older woman's shoulders. "We'll get it fixed," she promised. "I'm sure there's an auto body shop around here somewhere. It will be as good as new in just a couple of days."

Her grandmother nodded, but she could still see the doubt in the older woman's eyes. Ellie sighed, then urged her to come back into the motel room with her. This trip wasn't going how either of them had planned.

Chapter Six

Despite what had happened, Ellie found that she slept unexpectedly well that night. The long drive, combined with the sun, made it so that she was exhausted. Since the diner was already closed, she and her grandmother made do with a quick dinner of sandwiches and granola bars from the gas station across the street. Then, chatting for only a few minutes first, the two women got into their beds and, with the blinds closed and the air conditioning unit running, fell asleep.

Ellie woke up early, feeling disoriented at first. When she realized where they were, the memories of what had happened the day before came rushing back to her. The damage to the car that they were supposed to be transporting home was bad enough, but thoughts of the dead man were far worse. Damage to a vehicle was nothing compared to the loss of a man's life.

Trying not to wake her grandmother, she got up and showered quickly, then got dressed and went outside to look at the damage to the vehicle in the daylight. She bit back a sigh. While the damage seemed to be mostly cosmetic, she knew that there was no way they could drive all the way back to Maine with it like that. They would have to get it fixed here, before going back home.

She pulled out her cell phone reflexively, meaning to call around to see if there were any local car shops that might be able to handle the task of fixing the vehicle, then sighed when she saw the lack of phone service. She had forgotten that they were in a dead zone, which meant that she wouldn't even be able to call Russell.

Suddenly she remembered the phone on the desk between her and her grandmother's beds. Feeling silly, she returned to the room and picked up the handset, frowning down at the complicated instructions next to the phone. When she saw the big red letters that said *no out of area calls*, she sighed and put the receiver back down.

Maybe there is a phone I can use in the motel lobby, she thought. She left the motel room for a second time and walked over to the lobby, taking a wide detour around the room where the dead man had been found. When she let herself into the lobby, she realized that she had better see if she could extend their stay as well. She had rented the room for only one night, but it was looking like they were going to have to stay for another day or two at least.

She imagined herself sitting on a sunny beach down in Florida with her grandmother next to her, neither of them having a care in the world besides where they were going to eat lunch. Shaking her head, she sighed. There was no use in resenting or regretting the decision to go on a road trip. Neither of them could have possibly known what was going to happen, and it had sounded like a great idea to Ellie at the time.

Still, this was turning out to be more of an adventure than she had bargained for, and she was ready for it to be over.

Once again, the lobby was empty, but when she rang the bell on the front desk, a middle-aged man appeared within moments. He looked tired and his face was pinched with stress. She couldn't blame him, not considering what had happened the day before.

"My grandmother and I are renting a room number eleven," she told him, deciding to address the matter of their stay first. "We are driving the yellow vehicle that was in a collision yesterday, and we're going to need to find a way to get it fixed before we go home, so it looks like we'll have to stay for another couple of nights."

"Of course, of course," he muttered distractedly. "How many nights?"

"Let's start with two," she said. He nodded and punched something into the computer. "What number was your room again?"

"Number eleven," she said, watching as he finished registering them and preparing the machine to accept her card. Suddenly, something occurred to her. "That man who passed away yesterday... was he an employee here?"

The man across the counter looked up at her. "Richard? No. He was a health inspector." He frowned, seemingly lost in thought. "We knew him pretty well, though. He's been coming around yearly for the past decade."

"I'm sorry for your loss, then," she said.

He nodded. "That means a lot, Ms...."

"Ward," Ellie said. "Eleanora Ward."

"Charles Maple," he said, extending a hand to shake hers. "Sorry if I seem a little bit out of it. Nothing like what happened yesterday has ever happened here before. I've owned this motel for twenty years, and the worst we have ever had to deal with was some theft."

"I can't even begin to imagine what you're going through," Ellie said. "I'll just pay for this, then I'll stop bothering you."

"It's no bother," he assured her. "Once word gets around about what happened, goodness knows that we'll need the business. I don't know how we'll pull through this, to be honest. Poor Annie is a mess. I don't blame her; it was all I could do to even come in today."

"Is Annie your wife? Is it just the two of you that work here?"

"It's me and Annie, and a lady about your age named Sarah comes in sometimes to help out."

Ellie slid her card through the machine, thinking back to the woman she had seen yesterday passionately kissing the health inspector. What had that been all about? She hoped that the young woman was handling his death as well as she could.

After paying for their room, she made her way back and sat down on the bed, the sound of the shower running in the bathroom telling her where her grandmother was. She pulled out her cell phone again and paced around the room, looking for a spot with service. She had completely forgotten to ask the motel's owner if he had a long-distance landline that she could use, but didn't want to go back to the lobby so soon. It was obvious that he was having a difficult time, and she didn't want to bother him more than necessary.

After having no luck for a couple of minutes, she flipped through the book of Yellow Pages that was left on the desk between their beds and copied down the numbers of a couple of local auto shops. No matter how much the man's death was bothering her, she knew that it wasn't her responsibility to solve it, so she decided to focus on what she could do instead; finding a way to repair the car so they could make their way back to Kittiport.

"Do you want to go to that diner for breakfast?" her grandmother asked when she came out of the bathroom.

"Good morning to you, too," Ellie said, giving the older woman a small smile. "And sure, that sounds like a good idea." She'd had enough gas station food and fast food for a lifetime, and would be glad to sit at a real restaurant for a change.

It was lucky that the diner was so close by. She shot another glance at the damaged yellow car, then began walking across the parking lot with her grandmother. What was a short and easy walk for her, was a little bit more strenuous for the older woman. About halfway across the parking lot, Ellie had to let her grandmother – who had refused to bring her walker with her to the diner – lean on her. Letting Nonna take her arm, they walked the rest of the way together. Her grandmother, who had already asked all the questions she could think of about the man's death the evening before, was oddly silent as they made their way toward the restaurant. Ellie wondered what she was thinking, but decided to wait until they were seated to ask her. She didn't want her grandmother to waste her breath answering questions, not when she was already beginning to look so taxed.

Not for the first time, Ellie was suddenly struck by just how old the other woman was. It was so easy to forget her grandmother's age; most of the time, her mind was sharp, and despite the walker that she had to use occasionally now, she seemed to be able to get around pretty well on her own. Ellie felt a twinge of sadness. She wished that she had been able to know the woman when she had been younger and in the prime of her life. Her grandmother was an impressive person, and Ellie knew that there was no one else she would rather have beside her during a trip like this... other than her husband, of course. Suddenly, she missed him terribly, and swore to herself that she would find a way to call him as soon as possible.

Chapter Seven

The little diner was nicer inside than Ellie expected. It was empty, though she could hear voices in the kitchen, and smell the promising scent of something fried. Looking around for a sign that indicated whether or not they should seat themselves, she saw nothing, and with a shrug, led her grandmother to a table near the register. A moment later, a middle-aged woman came out, her hair pulled back in a tight ponytail, and a smile on her face that didn't quite reach her eyes. Ellie recognized her immediately. She was the same woman who had been kissing the health inspector in the motel.

"What can I get you?"

"I'll have orange juice, please," Ellie said.

"I'll have the same," Nonna said.

"All right, I'll go get your drinks while you look over the menus. The breakfast special this week is a double stack of pancakes with bacon, eggs, and hash browns on the side. We've also got some lovely French toast, though. It's my personal favorite."

Smiling, Ellie took the menus from her. She felt a sudden pang of homesickness as she thought of Papa Pacelli's in Kittiport. She always loved visiting other restaurants, of course, but nothing could compare to the pizzeria that she had worked in for the last two years. No matter how much she tried, she could never stop comparing her own restaurant to other people's restaurants. While the diner was nice and clean, and smelled absolutely wonderful, she privately thought that the pizzeria's atmosphere was much more welcoming.

Of course, she would never mention it. She tended to avoid talking about her own restaurant when she was out to eat. She didn't want people to worry that she was being judgmental. Most of the time, all she really wanted was to enjoy the food.

The waitress walked away to get their drink orders, and Ellie and Nonna pored over the menu.

Even though a lot of the options looked good, in the end, Ellie decided that she wanted to try the French toast. Russell had made it for her the day before the trip, and she thought it would remind her pleasantly of home.

When the waitress returned with their two glasses of orange juice, she and her grandmother were both ready to order. Her grandmother ordered a simple breakfast of an English muffin, eggs cooked Sunnyside up, and two sausage links. Ellie went all out with French toast, hash browns, and bacon.

"Coming right up," the waitress said, flashing them a quick smile. "Are you two new to the area? I think I've seen you before…"

This last was directed to Ellie. She nodded. "We're staying at Maple's Motel," she said. "We'll be here for a couple of days."

"Where are you from?" the other woman asked, her voice curious. "You have a little bit of an accent that I'm not familiar with. I never travel anywhere, so it's always neat to meet new people."

Ellie grinned at that. Apparently, she had picked up a little bit of the northern Maine accent in her two years in Kittiport.

"We're from Maine," Ellie explained. "We're taking a road trip back from Florida." The waitress let out a low whistle. "You're a long way from home. Well, I hope you enjoy our weather. You should come back for lunch or dinner; we serve the best hamburgers around. We're making a key lime pie for tonight that will knock your socks off, too."

Ellie agreed, thinking that they probably didn't have much choice. With the car out of service, they wouldn't be able to get anywhere unless they walked, and she didn't think that there were any other restaurants close by. Thinking of the car's current condition, she remembered the phone calls that she had to make, and she jumped up, following the waitress after giving her grandmother a hurried explanation about where she was going.

"Excuse me," she called out. The waitress, Sarah, turned around. "Do you have a landline that I could use? My cell phone doesn't get any service here, and I need to call my husband and see if I can find a body shop that will work on our car. Someone ran into it in the parking lot last night."

"Of course," the woman said. "Follow me, it's in the hallway between here and the kitchen. If you want, I can give you a recommendation for the best body shop in the area."

"Any recommendations would be great," Ellie replied.

She dialed Russell's number while the woman went into the other room to get the number to the auto shop for her. She breathed a sigh of relief when her husband answered. She hadn't been able to speak with him since yesterday morning, and she hadn't realized just how much she had missed him.

"It's me," she said when he answered. "I'm sorry, I don't have any cell phone service here, or I would have called you last night."

"Ellie," he said, breathing a sigh of relief. "I've been trying to call you. I was so worried."

"I'm sorry I didn't get in touch with you earlier. There was so much going on, and by the time we finally were done for the evening, I was just wiped out. Is everything okay there?"

"Everything's fine," he reassured her. "I stopped in at the pizzeria for dinner last night, and everything there is fine. The animals are doing well too. Of course, everyone misses you. How is the road trip going?"

Ellie took a deep breath, knowing that her husband wouldn't be happy with what she had to say, but at the same time, knowing that she had to tell him. "Actually, there has been a complication…"

Russell was silent for a long moment before replying after she finished her story. At last, he blew out another breath of air and said, "I have no idea how you keep finding yourself in these situations, Ellie."

Stung, she said, "It's not my fault. I wasn't even the one who found the body. That was Regina – the woman who ran into the car."

"I'm not saying it's your fault," he said soothingly. "I'm just worried about you, that's all. I hate the thought of not being able to keep you safe. It's my job to protect you."

Touched, Ellie said, "I know. And I wanted to call you as soon as it happened, but like I said, my phone didn't have any service. The phone in the motel room doesn't do long distance."

"Do you want me to fly out there?"

Ellie hesitated. The truth was, she would love to have Russell there, but logically, it didn't make sense. He would have to take time off of work, and she knew how difficult that was for him. Plus, he would also have to find someone to watch the animals, and she didn't know if their regular pet sitter would be available on such short notice. She didn't want to have to worry about the animals on top of everything else.

"No, it's fine," she said. "Nonna and I are just going to stay for a couple of days until the car is fixed, then we'll head straight home. I'll be okay."

"Well, maybe I can at least help from here. What did you say the man's name was? And what did the crime scene look like?"

"His name was Richard. I don't know his last name. It looked to me as though he had been stabbed, but I didn't get a good look at his wounds. He was just inside one of the motel rooms, and the door had been left open. I didn't see much besides…"

A crash sounded behind her, and she broke off midsentence, spinning around. The waitress, who had been on her way back out of the kitchen with a pad of paper and a tray with pancakes on it, had dropped everything on the floor.

"Richard?" The other woman's eyes were wide, and her face was pale. "Are you talking about what happened at the hotel last night? Richard was stabbed?"

Puzzled, Ellie nodded. She was distracted when Russell said something into her ear. "I'm going to have to call you back," she told him. "I just realized that the waitress here knew the victim, and might not know what happened. I'll call you as soon as I know what's going on."

She had time for a quick "I love you," then hung up the phone. The waitress was leaning against the wall, her face pale.

"Richard, he's the one that was hurt? I saw the police vehicles, but I was already on my way home and didn't stop to see what was going on."

Ellie nodded again. "I take it you knew him well?"

"I've been… Seeing him… On and off for the past couple of years," the woman explained. "I never would have guessed that the police were there for him, though. Is he okay?"

"He passed away," Ellie said softly, not sure how else to break the news. "I'm so sorry."

The other woman just stared at her, her breath hitching in her throat. "I think I need to sit down," she said at last.

Even as she led the waitress into the dining area and helped her sit down at the table with her and Nonna, she couldn't help but wonder why no one had told Sarah what had happened. If she worked at the motel part-time, certainly either Annie or Charles Maple would have mentioned his death. Was it possible that neither of them knew of her relationship with the health inspector? If that was the case, then the police might not know about it either. With any luck,

Sarah would have information that might help with the case. She would just have to convince the other woman to talk with the police first.

Chapter Eight

It took a while for the woman to calm down enough to speak. Ellie felt a surge of guilt. She had known that Sarah and Richard had been involved, but it hadn't even occurred to her that the waitress might not know about what had happened to the health inspector. It hadn't so much as crossed her mind to be careful about what she said on the phone to Russell.

"I'm sorry," the waitress managed to choke out at last.

"Don't worry about it," she told the other woman. "I'm just sorry that you had to find out this way. Will you be okay? Can you take the day off of work? You shouldn't have to stay here after all of this."

The other woman nodded her head. "I should be able to get the rest of the day off. I will just have to go and talk to my boss. We might need to call someone else in, but I can't... I just can't be here today." Ellie nodded her understanding. To lose someone close, unexpectedly like this, would be world shattering.

"Would you like to sit with us for a while longer, dear?" Nonna asked. "You shouldn't have to be alone right now."

Sarah shook her head. "I'll be fine. I just need some time. Thank you. I think it's better that I found out this way than if I heard on the news. I – I'll be all right."

She got up then, giving Ellie and Nonna tremulous smile, and vanished into the kitchen. A short while later, she reappeared, her purse in hand. She said nothing on her way out, but nodded at them. Ellie and Nonna set mostly in silence, both of them too stunned and saddened by the sudden turn of events to say much at all.

It wasn't long after that that a subdued looking waitress brought out their food. Even though Ellie had to admit that the French toast was fantastic, she could hardly concentrate on it. She wished that they had never chosen this motel to stop at. If they had only driven a few more miles down the freeway, they might have avoided all of this. *But Richard would have still died,* she thought. Everyone else would still be going through this, and it's so much worse for them.

After finishing their meal and leaving a sizable tip, the two of them walked back to the motel. Ellie, who's conversation with Russell had been cut short, made a beeline for the lobby after making sure her grandmother was comfortable in their room. She asked Mr. Maple if she could use the landline in the lobby to dial a long-distance number. He agreed after a moment's hesitation, then left her alone to call her husband.

She gave Russell a hurried explanation of what had happened. "I can try to call you this evening," she said. "I just wanted to get you caught up. Right now, I've really got to take care of the car. The sooner we get it into the shop, the sooner we can head home."

"Okay," her husband said reluctantly. "Just be careful, Ellie. I know that you might feel like you have some sort of responsibility to help these people, but just remember that the police can handle whatever comes up. All I want is for you and your grandmother to get home safely."

After saying her goodbyes to her husband, she grabbed the paper with the auto shop's number on it from her pocket and dialed the unfamiliar digits.

"Rob's Vehicle Repair," a man's voice said in answer.

"Hi," Ellie said, trying to pull her thoughts away from the murder and focus on the incident with the car. "I'm from out of state on a road trip, and someone ran into my car in a parking lot. We need to get it fixed before we can go home. I think it's mostly body damage. Do you think that's something that your shop can fix?"

"We do it all," the man on the other line said. "We can get it towed in and give you an estimate. Where are you?"

"We're at Maple's Motel. Do you know where that is?"

"I know the place," he said. "I'll bring a truck out to get it. What is the make, model, and color of the vehicle?"

She gave him the information, and he promised to be there soon. It should give Ellie some time to get the vehicle's insurance information prepared and for her grandmother to call the car's owner and let him know that they were taking it to the shop. She thought, not for the first time, about how much easier this would all be if only her cell phone worked. She had a feeling that she was going to be running back and forth from her room to the motel lobby quite a bit over the next couple of days.

The tow truck arrived not quite twenty minutes later. Ellie watched as the vehicle was loaded up, feeling a pang. It really was a beautiful car, and she hoped that they could fix it, so it looked as good as new.

She had a feeling that some parts might need to be special ordered, but they could always do that back in Kittiport as long as it was simply a cosmetic fix. All she wanted right now was for the car to be safe to drive back to Maine.

"Would the two of you like a ride into town?" Rob asked once he was finished. He had introduced himself to her as the owner of the auto shop, and she had taken an immediate liking to the friendly man. He had admired the car, and had seemed confident that he could get it fixed. "The shop is about fifteen minutes from here in another small town. It's not much bigger than this, but there are a few more shops. There is a bus that runs between the towns, so you can always get a ride back here later. The stop is right in front of the hotel."

Ellie exchanged a look with her grandmother. The older woman nodded, seeming to have regained her energy. Ellie was eager to get out of the motel. The idea of being stuck there without a vehicle for the next couple of days made her feel frustrated.

"That sounds nice," she said. "If you really don't mind giving us a ride."

"Not at all," he said. "Hop on in."

The drive to the next town didn't take long. Rob was chatty, telling them both stories about the area, which was where he had grown up. On their way into town, Ellie saw a rusted old sign that read Pottersville, population eight hundred. She felt a twinge of homesickness. Kittiport was nowhere near as small as this place, but there were still enough similarities that it made her miss home fiercely.

"Well, here we are," Rob said as he pulled into a parking lot. "The town is pretty small, you can walk just about anywhere. If you come back in an hour or so, I should have an estimate for you. It's a nice vehicle, and it's a real shame that it got damaged. What exactly happened?"

"Someone wasn't paying attention to where they were going and ran into it while it was parked," Ellie said, not wanting to go into details. If Rob hadn't heard about the man's death, she wasn't going to be the one to bring it up.

"Unlucky," Rob said, shaking his head. "A nice car like this, you really should park it out of the way. Vehicles get damaged in parking lots quite often. Anyway, I hope the two of you have a nice time."

With that, he hopped out of the truck and began to unload the vehicle. Ellie and her grandmother walked toward the sidewalk, looking up and down the street which was lined with small shops.

"Where do you want to go first?" Ellie asked her grandmother. The older woman was looking around the small town. There were a few tiny shops, a library, and what looked like a little park further down the road.

"Let's go shopping," the older woman said. "Maybe I'll pick up a souvenir. Not that I'll ever forget this trip, of course. I couldn't even if I tried."

Chapter Nine

Walking around Pottersville was pleasant, but tiring. It was a hot day, and Ellie hadn't thought to put on sunscreen before leaving the motel room. The bus didn't leave until three in the afternoon, which gave them plenty of time to explore the town, grab a quick lunch at the small café, and stop by Rob's repair shop to check on the car.

"Well, I can get it drivable if you give me a day or two. It won't look perfect, but once you get back to wherever you're going, you can do more expensive repairs. I'm guessing the two of you don't want to wait here for a couple of weeks while we order the parts, am I right?"

Ellie shook her head. "Just make it so we can get back to Maine safely. We can do the rest there."

The bus ride back to the motel was quick, and she could tell when they got off that her grandmother was tired. She didn't mind; she could really use a nap herself.

After spending the day outside under the hot sun, it felt wonderful to sprawl across the hotel bed with the blinds drawn and the air conditioner running at full blast. Ellie closed her eyes and her thoughts began to wander, still on the wrong side of sleep.

It sounded like the car would be fixed soon enough, then they would be headed home, and she would see Russell again. With her grandmother back home, things would be just like they had been the summer before. Well, not quite the same, she amended. She and Russell would be living in the house next door, which would be an interesting change for all of them. Still, it would feel as though things were back to normal.

She knew that she had managed to doze off, because when she opened her eyes again, the border of light around the curtains had darkened. She fumbled for her cell phone, which she kept close by out of habit, and checked the time. It was a little past six. She sat up, blinking the sleep out of her eyes. Somehow, she had managed to sleep for almost three hours.

She heard a soft snore from her grandmother's bed and knew that the older woman was still asleep. Even though her grandmother had been in mostly good spirits for the trip, Ellie knew that it must be taking a lot out of her. Considering how tired she was herself, she wasn't surprised. There was just something about traveling that seemed to suck all of the energy out of her.

Careful not to make too much noise, she slipped out of bed and went into the bathroom to refresh herself. She wanted to call Russell again and update him, which meant going back to the motel lobby. Inside, she rang the bell at the desk, and Mr. Maple came out of the backroom.

"What can I do for you?"

She wanted to ask after his wife, but decided not to. She knew firsthand just how private people who lived in small towns could be. She didn't want him to think that she was going to spread any rumors.

"Can I use your landline again? I need to make another call."

"Can't you just send an email?" He asked with exasperation. "Long-distance calls are expensive."

"I don't have any cell phone service here," she explained. "I don't have any way to send an email."

"Didn't you get a Wi-Fi code when you checked in?"

Ellie blinked. They had Wi-Fi here? "No, I didn't know that there was Internet here at all."

"Annie should have given you the code," he said, sounding exasperated. He scribbled something on a piece of paper. "Here it is. I'm afraid it's not the fastest Internet around, but it should do."

"Thanks." She smiled at him and took the piece of paper, feeling relieved. She hadn't realized how much she had hated being unable to communicate with her friends back home. At least this way, she would be able to send emails and check in with everyone. When she got back to the motel room, Nonna was still asleep, so she took her laptop out of her suitcase as quietly as possible and sat on her bed, opening the machine and laying it on her lap. It took her a couple of tries to get the code right, but at last she was connected to the Wi-Fi. Smiling, she pulled up her email service and sent a message to her husband, telling him that the car should be ready to go in a day or two, and promising that they would be back to Maine as quickly as possible. After that, she read the emails from Linda and Shannon, both of whom had sent her a couple of messages since she had last checked.

She replied to Linda's first, answering a couple of questions about her ideas for weekly specials. After that, she read through Shannon's email. She smiled when she heard how happy her best friend was. It sounded like her nephew was doing wonderfully, and Shannon had even begun going back to work part-time. It still felt strange to think that there was a tiny little baby back home that was related to her – if only by marriage. She had never had children herself, and was surprised at just how quickly she had fallen in love with the baby. She would do just about anything for him, and knew that Russell felt the same way.

"What time is it?" her grandmother asked from the other bed, her words froggy. Ellie finished sending her email and shut the laptop.

"Almost six-thirty," she said. "We slept about three hours. I can hardly believe it. We must have been really exhausted."

"I didn't expect a road trip to be this tiring," her grandmother admitted. "We should have just flown home. It's my fault that we are stuck here right now. I'm sure you want to get home and see your husband."

"Hey, I was already planning on spending the entire week with you," Ellie said. "Granted, this isn't what I had in mind, but I'm still enjoying our time together."

The older woman smiled at her, then slowly sat up. "Well, hopefully we will be able to continue our trip soon enough. What do you want to do for dinner? Should we go back to the diner?"

"I was thinking about ordering a pizza and seeing what's on the television," Ellie said. "Unless you feel like walking around more."

Nonna chuckled. "I definitely don't," she said. "Pizza it is."

Ellie smiled. Pizza held a special place in both of their hearts, thanks to Papa Pacelli's. She picked up the Yellow Pages and began flipping through the book, hoping to find a local pizza place that wasn't part of a chain. She always loved trying new pizza, and sometimes even found inspiration for her own restaurant.

"There's a place in here that looks like it might be good. I think it's nearby. The area code for the telephone number is the same, at least. It's called Brent's Pizza."

"They'll have to deliver," Nonna reminded her. "We don't have a car to go and pick it up."

"I'll give them a call and see if they do deliveries," Ellie said. "If they do, what toppings do you want?" Her grandmother thought for a moment, then shrugged. "I'll let you decide that. I trust you when it comes to pizza."

Ellie chuckled, then picked up the landline that was in the motel room, the one that they could only use for local calls. It didn't take her long to confirm that Brent's Pizza made local deliveries. Ellie place an order for a classic round pizza with sausage, tomatoes, and olives on it. As an afterthought, she ordered a couple of sodas for them as well. If they were going to have an evening in, they might as well live it up.

Chapter Ten

An hour later, she and her grandmother were seated on their respective beds, laughing together as they watched a sitcom on the television, both of them with slices of pizza on napkins in front of them. Ellie had managed to almost forget about Richard's death and the mystery of who had killed him, and was simply enjoying the time spent with her grandmother. If it wasn't for the niggling reminder that they were essentially trapped there, hundreds of miles away from home, with no way back unless the auto shop managed to fix the car, she might have almost been able to pretend that the vacation had gone as planned.

After finishing their pizza, which had been good, but not as good as Papa Pacelli's pizza, her grandmother made a speculative noise and frowned at the television.

PATTI BENNING

"This is about when I would make tea or hot chocolate to drink before bed," the older woman said. "But all this room has is coffee, and I don't want to drink caffeine right now."

"I'm sure the diner next door serves something," Ellie said. "I could walk over and see if you'd like."

"I'll join you," Nonna said, moving stiffly to get out of bed. Ellie, remembering how tired the older woman had been when they had finished with their walk around Pottersville earlier in the day, shook her head.

"I'm happy to go myself," she said. "I want to call Russell anyway, so I might take a little while."

"Of course," Nonna said, relaxing back into her bed with a smile on her face. "Young love…"

Ellie made a face, not bothering to point out to her grandmother that she was in her forties, so not exactly young. Although, she couldn't deny the love part.

She had mentioned calling Russell mainly to convince her grandmother to stay in the motel and rest, but now that she had mentioned it, it sounded like a good idea. Even though she didn't have any more

93

news about either the case or the car, it would be nice to say good night to her husband. She missed him more than she had imagined. He had become such an important part of her life, and it was strange to be going through something like this without him by her side. It wasn't until she left the hotel room that she realized it was fully dark outside. She felt a chill of apprehension, remembering too late that Richard's killer was still out there. For a moment, she considered going back into the motel room and telling her grandmother that she had changed her mind, but then shook herself out of it.

There were lights on in the parking lot, and the diner really wasn't that far away. The interior of the restaurant was glowing, and she could see the shapes of people moving around as waitresses took orders and customers ate and talked.

Still feeling tense, Ellie hurried across the parking lot. She was half expecting someone to jump out of the shadows and attack her, but she made it to the diner without anything happening. Feeling a little bit foolish – she really shouldn't let herself spook like this – she let herself in and took a seat, surprised to see the same waiters from the day before there.

After seeing Sarah's reaction to the news of Richard's death, she had expected the other woman to take at least a couple of days off from work. Immediately, she felt guilty. She knew that many people weren't as lucky as her, and often needed to work as many hours as they could simply to make enough money to pay the bills. She resolved to leave Sarah a large tip. The woman deserved it for coming in to work the day after she found out that her boyfriend had been killed.

"I heard you got your car taken in," the waitress said as she came up to Ellie's table. "I hope the two of you manage to get back home all right. It must be terrible, being stuck out here with nothing."

"It's been an adventure, that's for sure," Ellie said with a chuckle.

"So, what can I get you?"

"Do you serve tea?"

"We sure do. We have green tea, black tea, and chamomile."

"Can I get two chamomile teas to go?" She remembered the delicious key lime pie that they had eaten the evening before, and as an afterthought, added, "What is your dessert special tonight?"

"We've got strawberry rhubarb pie," the other woman said. "If you're heading back to the motel, I could even pack you up some ice cream on the side to go, so it doesn't melt."

"That sounds amazing," Ellie said. "I'll take the two teas, and two slices of pie with ice cream."

"Coming right up." The waitress flashed her a quick smile, then went into the kitchen, pausing for a moment to grab an empty soda glass off of one of the tables.

Ellie leaned back, looking around the diner, which was busier now than it had been when they had stopped in the day before. She realized that most of the people here must be regulars. *This place must be as much of a focal point as Papa Pacelli's is in Kittiport*, she thought. The thought made her feel very much like an outsider, which just added to her homesickness.

Even when she was in Florida, she had never felt so utterly far away from home. The Papa Pacelli's in Miami was a slice of familiarity, and Linda had become a close friend. Even her grandmother's condo, while not as familiar as the Pacelli house in Kittiport, felt more like home than their motel room. She hoped the car would be fixed soon. Being able to head home would be worth it, even if it meant that she would never know what had happened to Richard.

As if summoned by her thoughts of the car, Rob from the auto shop came through the diner's doors. She looked at him, surprised at the coincidence as he made a beeline toward the kitchen. He seemed to be familiar with the place, and she figured that he must be one of the diner's many regulars.

She was surprised when, a few moments later, he came out of the kitchen and walked straight over to her table. He greeted her with a grin, then took a seat across from her. "My wife told me you were waiting on some tea and pie. I thought I'd drop by to talk about your car. We actually managed to get most of the work done today. It's drivable, but it doesn't look pretty, and we are going to have to reattach the muffler before you can take it anywhere. It should be ready by tomorrow evening at the latest."

"Thanks," Ellie said automatically. It took her a moment to realize what he had said. His wife? Did he mean the waitress who had recommended it to her? She was surprised. Sarah had mentioned dating the health inspector; Ellie had never even considered that she might be married.

She stared at Rob, who looked just as friendly and open as he had before. Had he known about the affair? With a chill, she realized that if he had, then there was a very real possibility that he was Richard's killer. What better motive for murder could there be?

Richard was giving her an odd look, and she realized that he had asked her a question, but she had missed it. "Sorry, what was that?"

"I said, do you want us to send a line on the vehicle's information to a repair shop near where you live? If they can get a head start on ordering the parts, it will get fixed up a lot sooner."

"Oh, sure, thanks," she said. Almost immediately, she regretted it. Was it smart to tell this man who might be a killer what town she lived in? But it was too late to back out now. He was already promising to get the information from her tomorrow, and was standing up.

"I'll leave you in peace," Rob said. "I'd better go make sure Sarah is doing all right. I know that she knew the health inspector who died pretty well. She's never really lost anyone before, and it's tough for her." He frowned, a guarded look coming over his face. "Anyway, I'll see you tomorrow when you come to pick up the car."

With that, he walked away, heading back toward the kitchen. Ellie was left to watch him, feeling confused and concerned. She had so many questions, but had no one to talk to about it. This wasn't like Kittiport, where she knew everyone, and they all knew each other. She was the stranger here, and no one would take kindly to her gossiping about the locals.

As she gazed toward the kitchen, considering her options, a new concern occurred to her. If Rob had killed Richard in a fit of jealousy, did that mean that his wife might also possibly be in danger? As soon as she got her pie and tea, she resolved to go back to the hotel and see if she could use the landline again. She really needed to talk to her husband, but she didn't want to risk having a conversation with him about the case here, where anyone could overhear.

Chapter Eleven

Ellie stopped by the motel room to drop off the pie and chamomile tea. She grinned when she saw her grandmother's eyes twinkle at the sight of the delicious dessert and ice cream.

"I'd better put mine in the mini fridge," Ellie said. "I don't want it to melt before I get back."

"Where are you going?" her grandmother asked, looking up from the food with a puzzled expression on her face.

"I need to make a call," Ellie said. "I just realized that the person who is fixing our car is married to Sarah, that waitress from yesterday… And I saw her kissing Richard not even an hour before he died. I remember seeing the tow truck parked at the gas station across the street from the motel the day of the murder. I just want to talk to Russell to see what he thinks my next move should be."

"I should come with you," her grandmother said. "If you think I'm going to let you walk to the motel lobby alone in the dark after telling me all of this…"

"All I'm going to do is call Russell. The lobby is closer than the diner was, and there are lights all over. Besides, I'd rather you stay here. My cell phone doesn't work out here, so if something does happen, you will have to use the motel phone to call the police. It will be safer if you stay here and keep an eye out for me."

She waited while her grandmother frowned over this. After a moment, the older woman sighed. "I suppose you're right. But I'll be watching you through the window the whole time. If I see anything suspicious, anything at all, I'm going to make the call."

"I wouldn't expect anything less," Ellie said, giving the older woman a quick grin.

"And you really should stay and eat your pie first," Nonna said. "Because I'm not going to wait for you, and I don't want to eat alone."

Ellie chuckled. "That's a sacrifice that I'm willing to make. I'm still going, but I'll eat the pie first."

Somehow, her trip to the hotel lobby kept getting delayed. She spilled some pie filling on her shirt while eating, so she went to go change it, and realized that she had almost no clean shirts left. That led to her and her grandmother gathering all of their dirty clothes into a pile to be washed before they continued on their trip the next day.

"I'll need to stop and do laundry before we go," Ellie said. "I might as well do it tonight, I suppose. There are washers and dryers in the laundry room in the lobby, and I'm pretty sure they sell laundry soap up front. We might as well at least wear clean clothes."

"If you're going to do laundry right now, let me change into my other pair of pajamas. We might not get another chance to do laundry for a couple of days."

At long last, Ellie had a bundle of laundry in her arms and her motel room key in her pocket along with some change.

"Be careful," her grandmother said. "I'll be watching."

"I'm counting on it," Ellie said, smiling back at her.

She really didn't think that she was in any danger. Rob certainly hadn't acted as if he had any hard feelings toward her. In fact, she was beginning to be less certain that Rob had anything to do with the murder. It was all guesswork on her part. She still wanted to talk to Russell. If he thought that there was any merit and her concern that Sarah might be in danger from her husband, she would call the local police. If Russell told her that she was being silly, she would trust his judgment. She knew that no matter how protective he was of her, neither of them could stand by while an innocent person got hurt.

Still, even though she didn't think that she was in any real danger, it was nice to know that her grandmother was looking out for her. Even though it was well lit, the parking lot was a bit eerie at night. The lights were orange and flickered, making a strange buzzing sound that unsettled her. There were enough cars parked in the lot to create plenty of misshapen shadows. She wasn't a superstitious person, but she couldn't ignore the fact that someone had been violently murdered there just a few days beforehand.

She couldn't help it if she jumped when one of the shadows moved.

The motel lobby was empty as usual when Ellie got there. She looked around, knowing that she needed laundry soap, and saw some small individual packets of soap sitting on the front desk. They were fifty cents each, so she left her quarters on the counter and grabbed the packet. She wanted to use the landline, but she knew that the washer's cycle would take a good half hour, so she might as well get the clothes in as quickly as possible.

She made her way to the laundry room, shoving the door open with her shoulder and stepping inside, depositing the clothing in the open washing machine. The dryer was already running, and she hoped that whoever had a load of laundry in would come and empty it by the time she needed it.

She frowned at the jumble of clothing inside the washer; usually, she separated the whites from the colors, and the dark colors from the bright ones, but tonight she just couldn't be bothered. She would wash everything together in cold water and hoped for the best.

She poured in the detergent and stuck the quarters into their slots to start the cycle. She had just shut the top of the washing machine when the dryer behind her buzzed loudly. She jumped, letting out a yelp. Once she realized what had happened, she was immediately embarrassed. She really was on edge tonight.

She finished preparing the load of laundry and hit the button to start the cycle, then turned to leave the room just as the door opened. It was Mr. Maple, and he looked irritated to see her there.

"I'm just doing laundry," she said unnecessarily. "But since you're here, I was hoping to use the landline again before I go back to my motel room. I really need to call my husband."

An annoyed expression flashed across his face. "I'll have to add a surcharge to your bill."

"That's fine," she said. "It will be a quick call, I promise."

"Well, if you're paying the fee, I suppose it doesn't hurt anything," he said. "You know where it is. Make it quick, though. I think my wife is expecting a call from her sister."

"I'll be as quick as I can," she promised. She hurried by him, going to the phone behind the desk and dialing the familiar number. As the phone rang, it occurred to her that Charles and Annie Maple must live somewhere in the motel. They always seemed to be around, and the fact that Mr. Maple was doing his own laundry in the communal laundry room, made her think that they probably spent all of their time here. She wondered what it was like to own a motel. It must be neat to meet so many different types of people, but she thought that she preferred being able to get to know her customers like she did at the pizzeria.

Russell answered the call, interrupting her thoughts. "Ellie?"

"It's me," she confirmed.

"I thought I recognized the area code," he said. "How is everything going?"

"Well, we should be ready to go home by tomorrow evening," she said. "So, that's good news. I did want to talk about something else, though."

"Go ahead," he said. "I'm just about finished up with dinner, but the dishes can wait. I'm all yours."

She hesitated, looking around just to be sure that she was alone. She knew that gossip would spread like wildfire in such a small town, and if she was wrong about the whole thing, she didn't want to start any rumors about Rob or his wife. When she was certain that she was alone, she lowered her voice and told her husband about her suspicions about the waitress's affair and her husband's involvement in the murder. When she was done, Russell was quiet for a moment before responding.

"Are you sure you saw Rob on the day of the murder?"

"Well, I didn't see him exactly, but I saw a tow truck from his company. It was sitting in the gas station parking lot right across from the motel when I got here, but if I remember right, it was gone by the time the police arrived. I don't remember exactly when it left."

"Did you tell the police about it?"

"No. It barely even registered with me at the time."

"I think it's something that you should bring up with them before you leave. Just give the detective working on the case a quick call in the morning. Tell them what you told me. It does sound like there might be something there, but I wouldn't jump to conclusions just yet. I know it's difficult, but circumstantial evidence can be misleading."

"I know," she said, smiling slightly to think of all the times that she had nearly gotten in trouble just because she had been in the wrong place at the wrong time. "You don't think I should call him tonight?"

"It's late enough that you would probably be getting the detective out of bed, or interrupting time with his family. It's not an emergency, so it's probably fine if you wait until morning. You know how it is with you and me. If someone calls me about work while I'm supposed to be off duty, we both get unhappy."

She chuckled. "You have a good point about that."

"Will you email me once you've spoken to them? I'm just curious to hear what they have to say."

"I will," she promised. "And I'll give you a call right before we leave, as well. I can't wait to see you. I miss you."

"I miss you too," he said.

Smiling, she said her goodbyes and they hung up. Talking to Russell always made her feel better. He was logical, stable, and not prone to the same imaginative flights of fancy as she was. They were similar in many ways, but complemented each other in other ways. Once again, she was simply amazed at how lucky she was to have found him.

She was walking out from behind the desk when the door to the laundry room opened and she saw Mr. Maple come out with a laundry basket full of dried clothes. She smiled politely as she passed him, then froze and turned around, her eyes widening slightly. On the very top of the pile was a white shirt with dark, washed out rust colored stains.

Was it blood?

Chapter Twelve

Ellie's eyes went wide, and she opened her mouth to say something, but her foot got caught on the rug in front of the counter and she went sprawling across the floor. Mr. Maple dropped the laundry basket in surprise.

"Are you okay?"

"I'm fine," Ellie said quickly, struggling to her feet and wincing. Her knees ached where they had hit the floor. She was really getting too old to take falls like this.

"No, no, you should sit down," he said quickly, panic in his eyes. "I'll get you an ice pack and coffee or tea… please, just sit down."

"I'm fine," she repeated, more strongly this time. She couldn't figure out why he was reacting so strangely. Her eyes darted to the laundry that was laying across the floor, trying to find the bloodstained shirt. Had she imagined it? She knew that even if it did have blood on it, there were plenty of reasonable explanations. Maybe he was prone to bloody noses.

This is ridiculous, she thought. *Not two minutes ago I was convinced that Rob is the killer. Now, I think Mr. Maple is? It's not like his wife is the one having an affair with Richard. What could his motive possibly be?*

As Mr. Maple continued to go on and on about her sitting down, her eyes narrowed. While it was true that Mr. Maple's wife didn't have any sort of connection to Richard as far as she knew, he certainly did have a different sort of connection to the health inspector. If Richard was the motel's health inspector, then he might have the power to shut the place down, or at least give it heavy fines. The motel certainly looked as though it was running into the ground. What if Richard had found something that might close the motel down for good? That might be enough motive to drive Mr. Maple to murder.

"Can you walk?" the man asked, beginning to sound desperate. "Are you sure you don't want an ice pack?"

"I'm fine!" She snapped the words without meaning to. "Sorry," she said immediately, forcing herself to calm down.

"No, no, I'm sorry. It's just, someone got injured here last year and the rates on our insurance went way up. If there is another incident, we won't be able to afford to keep this place open. I just want to make sure that you really are okay. I know we can't survive a lawsuit."

She blinked. "I'm okay," she said, finding it uncomfortable to realize that the motel really was struggling. "I'm just going to go back to my room and lay down for a little bit."

"Okay..."

"Charles, didn't I tell you I was going to get the laundry?" an annoyed voice snapped from the door behind the desk. Ellie turned to see Annie Maple standing there, her hands on her hips. "Those are my personal things, and now they are spread across the floor for the whole world to see."

Glad that Mr. Maple's attention was no longer on her, Ellie began to back toward the door, only to freeze again when the woman's words hit home. Those were her clothes? That didn't explain the blood on the shirt at all. She tried to remember what Annie had been wearing the day she had first checked into the motel, but drew a blank. She had been too desperate to get a room and get off her feet to pay any attention to another woman's clothing.

"Sorry, dear," her husband said. "I was just trying to help. You seemed so upset ever since Richard was killed."

"This is my stuff," she muttered. "My shirt, where is my shirt…"

"What are you talking about?" her husband asked.

"I had a shirt in here that I wanted to keep track of, that's all," she said, biting her lip as she searched through the pile of laundry.

"It's all here, dear," he said. "I'll help you get everything sorted out. You just sit down. There is no need to worry."

He crouched down and began to pick up clothes. When he grabbed a white shirt and turned it over to begin folding it, Ellie saw the blood stains on the front of it. Her heart began to beat faster. What was going on?

She saw Mr. Maple freeze when he noticed the stains on the shirt. "Annie, is this blood? What happened? Did you hurt yourself?"

"I'm fine," his wife said quickly. "It's not my blood..." She slammed her mouth shut, eyes darting nervously to Ellie. Ellie saw Mr. Maple glanced down at the shirt, then looked back up at his wife. She took a hesitant step forward, not quite sure what to do. There was definitely something going on, but she couldn't put the pieces together quite yet.

"Whose blood is it, Annie?"

Annie's face went pale. "I don't know what you're talking about," she snapped. "I spilled some tomato sauce on myself, that's all."

"I've been married to you for thirty years. I know perfectly well what stains from tomato sauce look like by now, and this isn't it. This is blood, Annie, and a lot of it. What on earth happened?"

"Nothing!" the other woman shouted. Her gaze started to Ellie again. She seemed to forcefully rein her temper in. "Nothing, dear. It must just be mud or something. We can talk about it later."

Her husband ignored her, still frowning down at the shirt. Ellie wasn't sure what to do. Should she leave? Should she go back to the motel room and have her grandmother call the police? What if she left, and something bad happened to Annie or her husband? She still wasn't quite sure what was going on.

"Is it… Richard's?" Mr. Maple said, looking up at his wife and blinking slowly, as if he didn't want to believe it. And he inhaled sharply, but didn't say anything. He seemed to take her lack of denial as an answer. "Oh, Annie, what have you done?"

"He was going to close the motel down," the older woman said, her voice choked. Ellie's skin prickled at the confession. "I couldn't let him. I know how much you love this place. He told me exactly what was wrong with it, and I figured that if we had more time, we could fix it. If I was able to stop him from turning in the results, we might be able to keep this motel up and running."

"Oh, Annie…" The older man shook his head sadly. Ellie could see that his hands were shaking now. He let the shirt fall to the floor in a heap. "I can't believe you would do something like this."

He sounded heartbroken, and Ellie couldn't blame him. He had just mentioned that he had been married to Annie for thirty years. Ellie tried to imagine what it would be like to have been with someone for so long, only to have them do something like this. She couldn't fathom it.

"I did it for you," the woman said, as if that was supposed to make things better. "You love this place so much. I couldn't let him take it from you."

"I can't believe you killed someone," Mr. Maple said, his voice breaking. He got to his feet and took half a step back, then seemed to remember that Ellie was there because he snapped his head around to look at her, his eyes widening.

Chapter Thirteen

"I'll... I'll go call the police," Ellie said, taking stumbling steps backward, desperate to get out of there.

"Charles, don't let her go," Annie said, the woman's voice now tinged with panic. "They'll send me to prison. We have to stop her." When her husband hesitated, she added "Think of what I did for you. Don't let it be for nothing. You have to help me keep her from saying anything."

"You're insane," Ellie bit out. "He's not going to help you kill me just because it..."

She broke off, seeing a strange sort of resolve filling the man's eyes. Her blood turned to ice in her veins. After thirty years of marriage, why would she expect Charles Maple to suddenly turn against the woman he loved and let her spend the rest of her life in prison? For some people, love really did conquer all.

"I should never have let you use that darn landline," he muttered, mostly to himself. Ellie, beginning to realize that she might be in real danger, started to backpedal. Luckily, she was near the door, and the older man didn't seem to have quite come to a decision yet. Ellie pushed through the door, then turned and ran back toward their motel room.

She didn't stop running until she was inside, shutting the door behind her and throwing the deadbolt. Her grandmother was standing by the window, staring at her in shock.

"Are you all right?"

"I'm fine," Ellie panted. "But we need to call the police, right now."

Her grandmother's eyes widened, but instead of questioning her, she reached over to the desk and picked up the phone off of its cradle. She typed the three digits into it and Ellie listened with bated breath as it began to ring.

"Hello?" she heard the dispatcher say. Nonna handed the phone to Ellie.

"We're at the Maple Motel," she said, quickly giving him the closest intersection. "Please, send someone right away. I think someone's going to try to kill me."

"Please stay on the phone, ma'am. Why do you think someone is going to try to hurt you?"

Before Ellie could answer, the room went dark and the phone went dead. She could tell by the echoing silence that the power had been shut off. The Maples must have cut the power to the entire building in an effort to keep her from contacting the outside world.

"This is bad," Ellie murmured, fear rushing through her. It was different than the fear that she had felt while listening to the older woman's confession. This was a more primitive fear, the fear of being trapped. There was only one exit in the room, and no other way out.

"The door is dead bolted, they can't open that with a key," her grandmother said. "We can pull the curtains shut and just wait for someone to save us."

"We don't even know if the police are on their way," Ellie said. "They might have thought it was a prank call. I can tell that the dispatcher didn't believe me. And besides, I'm pretty sure that they have a master key that can open any of the locks."

"Then what do we do?" her grandmother asked.

Ellie looked out the window, staring at the diner across the parking lot. The lights were still on inside, even though she thought that the restaurant was probably closed by now. There was a chance that Sarah or another employee might still be there, cleaning up. Then she looked back at her grandmother and squashed down the plan that was forming in her mind. There was no way that she was going to leave the older woman behind, and she knew that her grandmother could never make a run across the parking lot.

"Ellie, you have to go," the older woman said, having followed the direction of her gaze.

"It's too far," Ellie whispered. "We would never beat them to the diner."

"We wouldn't," her grandmother agreed. "But you would."

124

"No, Nonna, I'm not leaving you…"

"You have to," the older woman said. "You have to go call for help and make sure that the police are on their way. Just go and run across the parking lot before those two psychos try to kill us in our motel room."

"But what if they come after you instead?"

"I think it's you they're after, not me. I'll be perfectly fine. And besides, you need to get home to Russell, Ellie. I'm not going to be the reason my granddaughter dies. Don't risk your life for mine."

Ellie felt a lump in her throat. She loved her grandmother, so of course she would risk her life for the older woman's. But she couldn't deny that her grandmother's plan was the only one they had. They needed to make sure that the police were on their way, and the only way that they could do that was at the diner.

"Promise me that you'll be careful," Ellie said. "Lock the door when I leave and hide as best you can."

"I will," Nonna said. "You promise me that you'll run as fast as you can without looking back."

The two of them stared at each other for a second, then Ellie pulled the older woman into a tight hug before hurrying toward the motel room door. She knew that every second counted. It wouldn't take the Maples long to come and try to ensure her permanent silence. Taking a deep breath, she yanked the door open and stepped out it without looking behind her. It wasn't just her life that was on the line now, it was her grandmother's as well.

She didn't get far. The older couple must have been waiting for her. The instant she stepped out of the motel room, she felt something strike the back of her knees, and she fell down, hitting the same bruises that she had first made when she tripped in the lobby. She hissed in pain. If she survived until tomorrow, she was going to be quite sore.

"Annie," she heard Mr. Maple cry out. She twisted her head around, trying to see what was happening. If this was it, then she wanted to see her attackers face to face.

Annie was standing above her, holding a crowbar. Slightly behind her was her husband, looking pale and shocked… and not at all like he was prepared to bash her brains in.

"We have to make sure she won't tell anyone, Charles," Annie snapped. "Help me with this."

Annie raised the crowbar higher, tightening her grip on it. Ellie flinched, reflexively holding up her hands in a weak attempt to shield herself. Out of the corner of her eye, she saw the motel room door opening, and felt her heart skip a beat. She did not want her grandmother out here for this.

She saw Annie tense and at the last second decided to try to dodge the blow. She rolled away, hearing the crowbar clang against the asphalt only inches from her head. It hit hard enough that she knew that if she had tried to block it with her hands, she would have suffered multiple broken bones as a consequence.

"I'm not letting you tear apart my life," Annie said. "I'm not going to lose the motel, and I'm not going to lose my husband or my freedom. I won't let anyone stop me."

Ellie scrambled backwards, trying to get away from the crazed woman. She was raising the crowbar again, and her husband was still standing back, his eyes wide and his face pale.

She was just about to brace herself for the next attack when her eyes went wide at the sight of Nonna standing behind Annie with her walker raised over her head. The other woman must have seen her gaze, because she spun around just a split second too late. Nonna brought the walker down, the aluminum frame clashing against the crowbar. She hadn't dealt the blow with much force, but the shock of it had been enough that Annie released her grip on the crowbar and let it fall to the ground. She stumbled backward into her husband.

"Hurry, Ellie," Nonna said. "Come here."

"Don't try to hide," Annie spat at them. "You can't call the police. We shut the power off. There's nowhere else to go. I'm not letting you tell anyone what I did."

She tried to take a step forward, but now Ellie saw Mr. Maple's hand on her arm. The older woman looked back at her husband in surprise. He simply shook his head at her.

"That's enough, Annie. I'm not a killer. I didn't think you were either, but I'm not going to let you do this to anyone. They did nothing wrong."

"Don't you get it? I'll go to prison if we let them get away. You'll never see me again."

"I would rather be married to a woman in prison than be married to a murderer."

He seemed to be purposefully ignoring the fact that his wife had already killed one person, but Ellie wasn't about to interrupt to point out the flaw in his logic. She saw Annie's breath catch and tears appear in the other woman's eyes.

"All we have to do is make them disappear, then we can have our life back to normal," she said, her voice barely a whisper. "I don't want to go to prison, Charles."

"I'm not letting you do this," her husband said sadly, pulling her back so that he was hugging her, restraining her even more securely than when he had simply had his hand on her arm.

Ellie realized that she could hear sirens off in the distance. The dispatcher must have believed her enough to send police to their location, and she felt a rush of relief. Slowly, keeping a wary eye on the Maples, she got to her feet, moving to stand by her grandmother. She was shaking, with adrenaline still rushing through her body. She didn't think that she had ever been so close to death before, and she certainly didn't want to ever be so close to it again.

Epilogue

"We're in Maine," Ellie said, smiling over at the older woman next to her. Nonna beamed, looking around.

"We really are going to make it home today, aren't we?"

"Yes, we will," Ellie said. She couldn't wait to see Russell again. So much had happened during the trip. The murder, the affairs, even the car wreck. She wanted to tell her husband about everything in minute detail.

Thinking about Russell made her think about Charles and Annie Maple, as well as Rob and Sarah. She couldn't imagine ever betraying Russell by murdering an innocent person or having an affair. Even if her own morals and beliefs prevented her from doing anything of the sort, she knew that the thought of Russell's great disappointment in her would be enough to keep her from doing anything of the sort. She loved him, and she never wanted him to look at her and see a bad person.

Luckily, compared to the beginning of their trip, the rest of it had seemed uneventful. She and her grandmother had spent a long couple of days driving up the East Coast of the United States in the still somewhat damaged car. The first day after leaving the Maple Motel they had both been quiet and brooding. They had witnessed a thirty-year marriage get destroyed, had helped solve the murder, and Ellie had found herself face to face with a dead man yet again. The latter seemed to be becoming a habit, and it was a habit that she wanted to get out of, quickly.

With any luck, this coming summer would be a relaxing one. She would have her grandmother living right next door to her, and Russell had promised to take weekends off whenever he could. With him, the animals, and her best friend, she knew that she would never be lacking company. The pizzeria was bound to be busy, and with the new construction beginning on the hotel that her friend Joanna's husband was building, the little town was sure to be getting its fair share of extra tourism.

No matter how busy it was, as long as she could avoid getting involved in any cases, she was sure that it would be relaxing compared to the last summer. She would be at home with the people she loved and trusted. She could forget about dead bodies, murders, and betrayal. If there was one thing that she was sure of, it was that she could trust the people that she had come to think of as family.

Made in the USA
Lexington, KY
02 August 2018